FOR MY
PARENTS

copyright © 2008 by Kevin Waldron

All rights reserved. No part of this book may be reproduced, transmitted, or stored in an information retrieval system in any form or by any means, graphic, electronic, or mechanical, including photocopying, taping, and recording, without prior written permission from the publisher.

First U.S. edition 2010

Library of Congress Cataloging-in-Publication Data is available.
Library of Congress Catalog Card Number 2009015137
ISBN 978-0-7636-4549-6

10 11 12 13 14 15 TLF 10 9 8 7 6 5 4 3 2 1

Printed in Dongguan, Guangdong, China

This book was typeset in Bokka-Solid and Aunt Mildred.
The illustrations were done using digital media.

Edited by Ruth Martin

TEMPLAR BOOKS

an imprint of Candlewick Press
99 Dover Street
Somerville, Massachusetts 02144
www.candlewick.com

# MR. PEEK
## AND THE MISUNDERSTANDING
## AT THE ZOO

# KEVIN WALDRON

templar books
an imprint of Candlewick Press

AT THE STROKE OF 9 AM, MORE OR LESS,
MR. PEEK THE ZOOKEEPER
GETS READY TO DO HIS ROUNDS.
HE PUTS ON HIS FAVORITE JACKET.
IT MAKES HIM FEEL VERY IMPORTANT.

HE NOTICES THAT IT IS VERY TIGHT.
THEN ONE OF THE BUTTONS POPS OFF!
THIS IS NOT A GOOD START TO HIS DAY,
BUT HE SETS OFF NONETHELESS.

"It's only a button!"

"Oh, woe is me! You're getting very fat,"

MR. PEEK SAYS TO **HIMSELF**, NOTICING THE BULGE IN HIS JACKET.

THE **HIPPO** OVERHEARS AND THINKS THE REMARK IS INTENDED FOR **HER!**

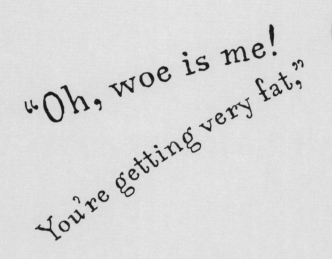

"All that terrible food you eat will be the end of you!"

MR. PEEK PROCLAIMS AS HE PASSES THE PENGUIN POOL. HEARING THIS, THE PENGUINS ALL LOOK AT ONE ANOTHER **IN HORROR.** THEY HAD **JUST** FINISHED BREAKFAST!

"Why, you're sweating just doing your rounds,"

MR. PEEK SAYS TO **HIMSELF** AS HE APPROACHES THE **BEAR** CAVE.

"You stink!"

HE **EXCLAIMS**.

"You're getting old, too. Look how wrinkly you are,"

DECLARES MR. PEEK **TO HIMSELF**
AS HE PASSES THE ELEPHANTS.

"If they think you're too old for this job, they'll fire you!"

HE SAYS WITH A SIGH AS HE PASSES THE **CROCODILE** PIT.

"They're **always** watching!"

MR. PEEK CHECKS ON THE **MONKEYS,**
MUTTERING TO HIMSELF,

"They're all out to get you."

"You can't turn your back for a moment! But maybe it won't even come to that,"

HE SAYS AS HE **SULKS** NEAR THE **TORTOISE'S** GARDEN.

"You could get run down by a rhino tomorrow!"

"Would anybody even care?"

MR. PEEK ASKS HIMSELF ALOUD,
SURROUNDED BY THE GIRAFFES.

"None of the animals even like you!"

*"Oh, woe is me!"*

MR. PEEK CONTINUES, FEELING VERY SORRY FOR HIMSELF.

TURNING A CORNER, HE SEES HIS SON, **JIMMY,**
SWEEPING THE PATH IN A **VERY LARGE** JACKET
THAT REACHES **DOWN** TO THE GROUND.

MR. PEEK AND JIMMY SWAP THEIR JACKETS.
JIMMY'S JACKET IS **MISSING A BUTTON**,
BUT HE CAN SEE THE FUNNY SIDE OF IT.
MR. PEEK IS VERY RELIEVED.

"See you at home for lunch, son,"

HE SAYS **CHEERILY**,
AND SETS OFF AGAIN.

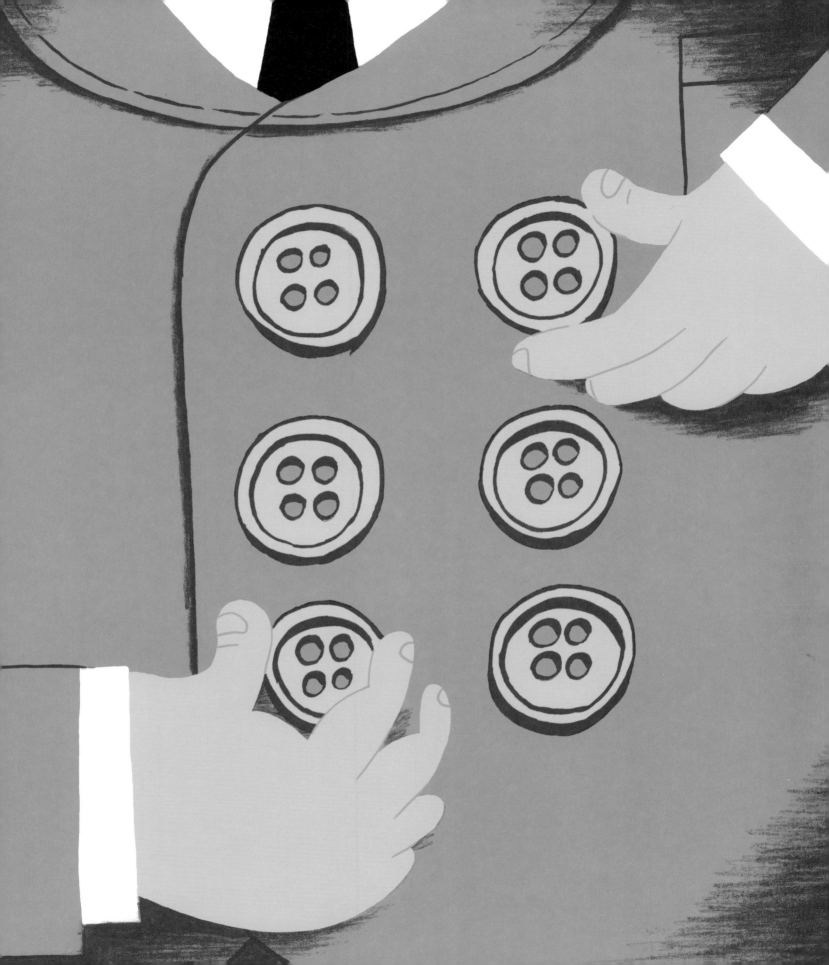

"I guess you're **not so fat** after all!
In fact, you're in pretty good shape
for someone your age,"

MR. PEEK SAYS TO HIMSELF
AS HE MAKES HIS WAY BACK HOME.

THE HIPPO WAS MUCH HAPPIER
WITH **THAT**.

"You don't smell bad at all.
No need to worry about that."

A **REASURED** BEAR
STEPS OUT OF HER CAVE.

"You're not too wrinkly, either.

You look fine just the way you are."

THE **ELEPHANTS** FLAP THEIR **LARGE** EARS AND TRUMPET WITH DELIGHT.

"You were foolish to think that they are always watching you!"

WHEN THE CROCODILES **HEAR** THIS,
THEY **RELAX** AND **LAUGH** AT THEMSELVES.

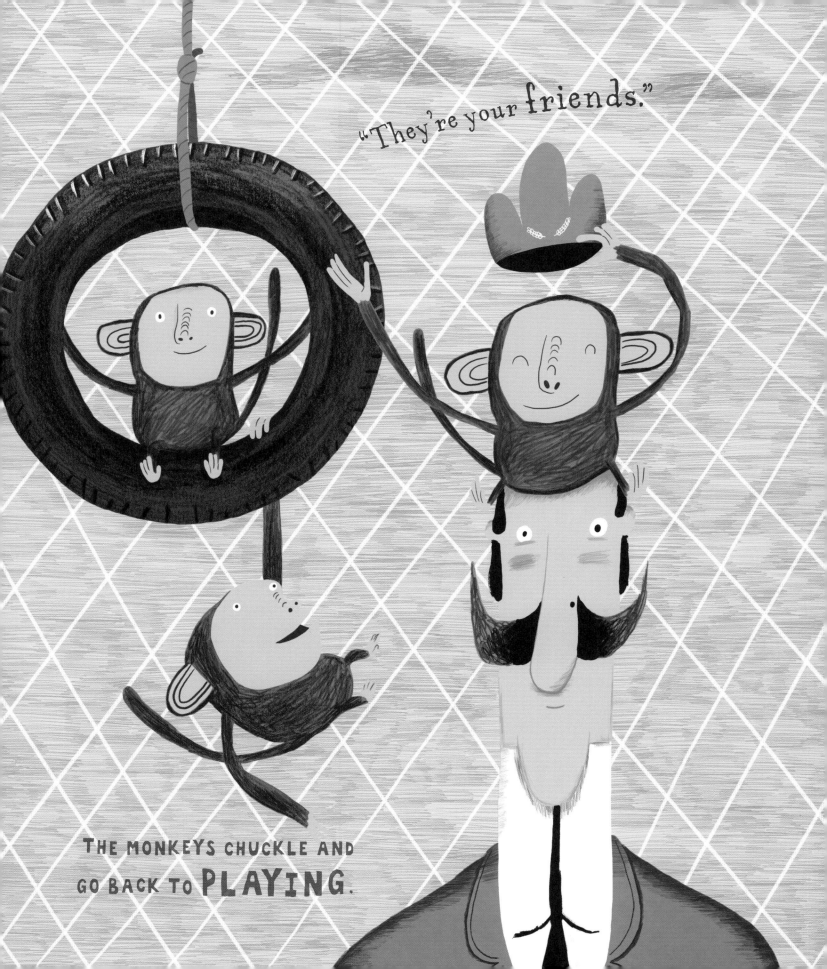

"You're fit and healthy. Why worry?"

"PHEW!"

THE **GIRAFFES** WERE STILL FEELING **BLUE**
UNTIL MR. PEEK PASSED BY AND SAID,

"All the animals
are like family to you.
There is no reason
to **doubt** that."

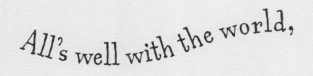
All's well with the world,

THOUGHT MR. PEEK, **PLEASED** TO SEE
THE ANIMALS LOOKING SO CHEERFUL.
HE HAD THOUGHT THEY LOOKED A
LITTLE **GLUM** EARLIER ON.

MR. PEEK PROMISED HIMSELF THAT HE
WOULDN'T GET **SO CARRIED AWAY** AGAIN.
HE REACHED INTO HIS POCKET
FOR HIS KEYS . . .

# BUT THEY WERE **NOT** THERE!

"Oh, poop! Those mischievous monkeys must have picked my pockets!"

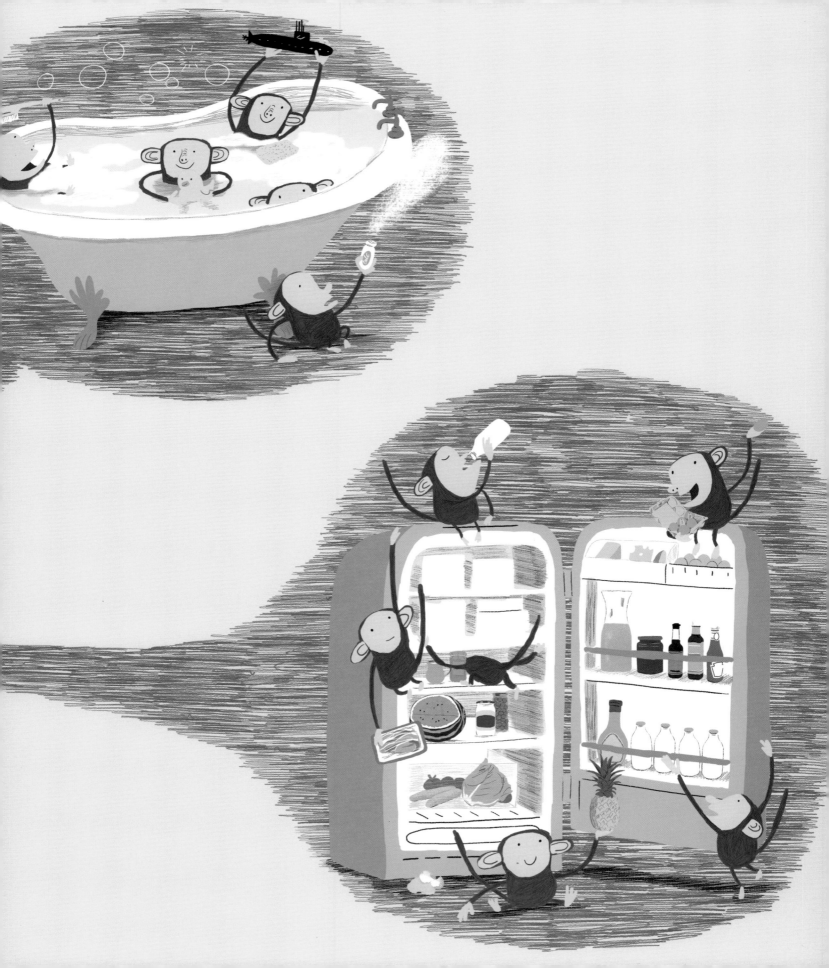

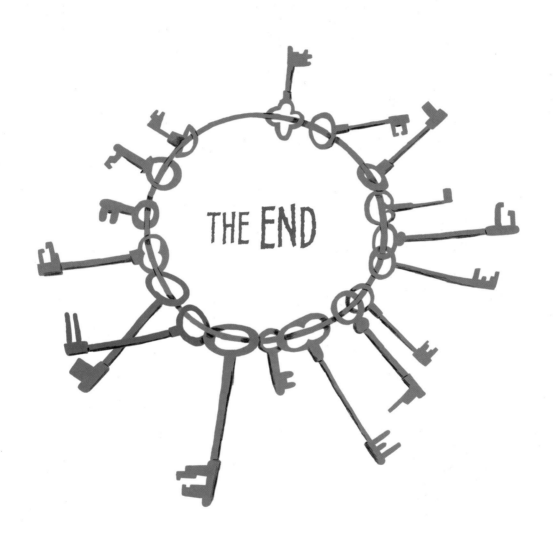

THE END